Dear Parent:

Your child's love of reading starts here!

Every child learns to read in a different way and at his or her own speed. Some go back and forth between favorite books again and again. Others read in order. You can help your young reader grow more confident by encouraging his or her own abilities. From books your child reads with you to the first books he or she reads alone, there are I Can Read Books for every stage of reading:

SHARED READING
Basic language, word repetition, and whimsical illustrations, ideal for sharing with your emergent reader

BEGINNING READING
Short sentences, familiar words, and simple concepts for children eager to read on their own

READING WITH HELP
Engaging stories, longer sentences, and language play for developing readers

READING ALONE
Complex plots, challenging vocabulary, and high-interest topics for the independent reader

I Can Read Books have introduced children to the joy of reading since 1957. Featuring award-winning authors and illustrators and a fabulous cast of beloved characters, I Can Read Books set the standard for beginning readers.

A lifetime of discovery begins with the magical words **"I Can Read!"**

Visit www.icanread.com for information
on enriching your child's reading experience.

Especially for Elliot Henry,
Ethan Charles, and Maverick Roy!
—A.S.C.

Biscuit and Friends: A Day at the Aquarium
Text copyright © 2023 by Alyssa Satin Capucilli.
Illustrations copyright © 2023 by Pat Schories.

Library of Congress Control Number: 2022933113
ISBN 978-0-06-291007-3 (trade bdg.) — ISBN 978-0-06-291006-6 (pbk.)

Book design by Marisa Rother

23 24 25 26 27 CWM 10 9 8 7 6 5 4 3 2 ❖   First Edition

I Can Read!

BEGINNING 1 READING

Biscuit
and Friends
A DAY AT THE AQUARIUM

story by ALYSSA SATIN CAPUCILLI
pictures by ROSE MARY BERLIN
in the style of PAT SCHORIES

HARPER
An Imprint of HarperCollinsPublishers

"Stay here, Biscuit.

We're going to the aquarium.

We'll see all kinds of fish,

and some sea turtles, too!

We'll be back soon!"

Biscuit watched the little girl

and her friends set out on their way.

Woof, woof!

Biscuit didn't want to wait!

Could he go along?

Woof!

Biscuit had never been

to the aquarium.

Which way could it be?

Biscuit sniffed here and there.

He passed the school and pond.

He passed the library and park.

Biscuit sniffed again and again,

until . . .

Woof, woof!

Biscuit found the aquarium at last!

He couldn't wait to go inside.

The aquarium was filled with fish
of every size and color!
Woof!

Biscuit saw sharks swimming by.

He saw tall tanks of jellyfish.

But it wasn't long before he found

what he was really looking for!

Woof, woof!

"Oh, Biscuit!

How did you find your way here?"

asked the little girl.

Woof, woof!

"Follow us now, Biscuit.
There's a lot to see
at the aquarium."
Woof, woof!

"Over here, Biscuit.

Let's stop at the touch pool."

Woof!

But Biscuit was not ready to stop.

He wanted to see the sea turtles.

The sea turtles wanted to see him, too!

Woof, woof!

Just then, Biscuit heard

a loud barking sound.

What could it be?

Woof!

Biscuit hurried past more fish.

He ran outside

and saw a crowd waiting.

The barking was getting closer!

Bark! Bark!

Woof, woof!

"Funny puppy," said the little girl.

"I knew you'd find the seals

and the sea lions!

Look! Here comes their trainer."

Woof, woof!

It was fun to see the trainer feed
the seals and the sea lions.
The seals swam gracefully
through the water.
The sea lions barked and barked.

Just then the trainer looked

here and there.

Was something missing?

Woof, woof!

Biscuit saw just what the trainer
was looking for.
He gave it to her at once.
Woof, woof!

"Thank you!" said the trainer.

"Seals and sea lions need

plenty of playtime!"

"A day at the aquarium
wouldn't be the same
without you, Biscuit,"
said the little girl.

"I'm glad you found your way.

I think we all are!"

Bark! Bark!

Woof, woof!